DEREK THE
...ESSED VIKING
in...

...'d be a Viking?

...ITH BRUMPTON

ORCHARD BOOKS

OTHER BOOKS BY KEITH BRUMPTON
(yes, I know you haven't read this one yet, but suppose it suddenly burst into flames?)

Dinosaur World Cup
A Dinosaur's Book of Dinosaurs
Ig and Tig's Trip to Earth
The Mystery of the Missing Moggie
The Mystery of the Dog with 1,000 Disguises
The Mystery of the Great Sheepdog Swindle
The Mystery of the Dachshund Diamonds
· DEREK BOOKS ·
The Dragon from the Black Lagoon
Nice Crown, shame about the Throne
Kidnapped by Ice Maidens

To find out more about Keith Brumpton's books,
visit his website at:
http://www.okukbooks.com/kbrumpton/

Contents

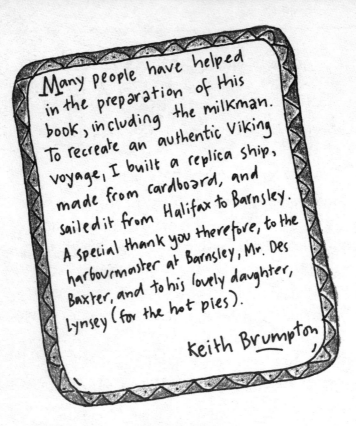

Many people have helped in the preparation of this book, including the milkman. To recreate an authentic Viking voyage, I built a replica ship, made from cardboard, and sailed it from Halifax to Barnsley. A special thank you therefore, to the harbourmaster at Barnsley, Mr. Des Baxter, and to his lovely daughter, Lynsey (for the hot pies).

Keith Brumpton

ORCHARD BOOKS
96 Leonard Street, London EC2A 4RH
Orchard Books Australia
14 Mars Road, Lane Cove, NSW 2066
First published in Great Britain 1997
First paperback publication 1998
Copyright © Keith Brumpton 1997
The right of Keith Brumpton to be identified
as the Author and Illustrator of this Work has been
asserted by him in accordance with the Copyright,
Designs and Patents Act, 1988.
A CIP catalogue record for this book is
available from the British Library.
1 86039 356 X (hbk)
1 86039 600 3 (pbk)
Printed in Great Britain

THE DARK AGES

...A time of chaos and of bumping into things. A time when monks trembled, and not just because the wind was blowing up their cassocks.

The Vikings had just begun to voyage from their homelands in the far north. These were no mere pleasure trips. The Vikings came to destroy. To plunder. And to terrorise. And that was if they were in a good mood.

Among all the Vikings, one name has recently come to light, his stories miraculously preserved in an old Danish bog.

The sagas of Derek the Depressed are like no other in the Viking world. They tell not of bravery and adventure, but of cowardice and confusion. Of a seven-foot-tall warrior who suffered from seasickness and whose legs couldn't fit under the oars. A man who considered swords "too sharp to be safe."

Now, for the first time, the story of Derek the Depressed Viking can be told in full, starring (in order of cowardice)...

 Derek Drodnodrott

 Frank the Seagull

 Princess Anka

 Chief Harald Hafnomörssy.

Chapter One: Fish and Ships - in which we meet our hero for the first time.

It was only seven o'clock in the morning, but already the Viking village of Upper Elkshead was filled with the sound of men preparing for battle.

Ships were being dragged out in to the water, sails unfurled, armour polished, and shields tested for woodworm. The master oarsmen were checking their routes.

The Vikings, as you probably know, were a bloodthirsty lot, and the Vikings of Upper Elkshead were worse than most. Their chief, Harald Hafnomörssy, had won several awards for bad behaviour at sea and being nasty to defenceless monks.

Every month these Vikings set out to loot, burn and pillage. The sight of their ships caused terror even among the short-sighted. And now Chief Harald planned a new expedition which would involve sailing across the North Sea to Northumbria and looting the local monastery. The plan proved popular with everyone in the village. Well, almost everyone...

 Derek the Depressed Viking →

Derek Drodnodrott hated the Viking life. There were three main reasons:
1. He hated going on long voyages because he got seasick (pretty disastrous since Vikings went almost everywhere by boat!)

2. Because he was so tall, his legs couldn't fit under the oars, so he had to stand up for the whole trip which made him feel faint.

3. Worst of all, Derek didn't like battles.

Now, a Viking who doesn't like battles is a bit like a reindeer who doesn't like snow. But try as he might, Derek couldn't get up any enthusiasm for the old hand-to-hand combat. The swords were too sharp, he felt, and the shields too small. Maybe if someone invented a shield that would cover your whole body...

DEREK

Unfortunately nobody had, so Derek the
Depressed remained something of an outcast
in the village. Even the girl he loved, the

Chief's daughter, Anka, thought it was time he got a grip.

Anka was too kind to say anything, though, and had come to the shore to wave Derek off. She stood next to Derek's mother who was just helping him fasten on his broadsword.

"Have you got everything? Helmet?"

"Yes, Mum."

"Shield?"

"Yeah."

"Clean socks."

"Mu-m!"

"OK. Off you go then, and be a bad boy."

"I'll try."

"Kiss Mummy."

The other Vikings laughed as Derek waved goodbye to his mum and Anka, and took up his usual place next to the main mast.

Olaf Dednafffellur was a tall, blond-haired beserker* who teased Derek more than most.

Deggsie looks sea sick already. Tch! I don't know why we bother to bring him. He's a coward from helmet to toe!

Derek didn't reply. There was no point in norse-ing a grudge.

Chief Harald suddenly leapt to the front of their ship, *Serpent's Breath*, and raised his mobile horn. He blew a long, high note,

(*The beserkers were particularly fierce warriors. They wore bear skins – no, not bare skins, *bear* skins – and went absolutely BESERK when they saw the enemy. Best avoided.)

slightly out of tune, which echoed down the misty fjord, and with a great cry of excitement from the shore, the fleet of Viking ships set sail.

Derek looked up at the sky and hoped that the weather would stay fine. It was going to be a lon-n-ng trip.

Chapter Two: Thunder Bird - in which Derek gets a new gull-friend.

It was night time now, and the skies were as black as the devil's toothpaste. Derek felt a strange sensation in his stomach. Perhaps it was the chocolate moose he'd just eaten. Those moose were big creatures. Or perhaps it was from fear of the battle ahead.

The ship began to bob about on the waves. It was rolling back and forth like a penguin at a roller-disco. Derek clutched on to the mast and hoped that no one would notice how ill he was feeling. He looked up and saw the stormy skies being lit by occasional steaks of lightning. Great prongs of light seemed to move closer and closer towards the mast-head where he was standing...

Derek wished he was back at home with his Beowulf annual and a cup of hot goat's milk. The other Vikings had covered themselves with their cloaks and were trying to snatch a few hours of sleep before the next leg of their trip.

Derek found he couldn't sleep. Not even when he tried counting reindeer. At this moment, just when his spirits were as low as the attendance at a Scarborough United football match, a large seagull came and landed with a thwack! on the deck next to him.

At first Derek thought it had come to look for fish - that's usually the only reason anyone enjoys a seagull's company. But to

Derek's surprise, the gull took a couple of
steps closer and began to speak.

Thor* be with you,
Derek. My name is
Frank and I'm your
guardian seagull.

Derek couldn't quite believe his ears.
He'd never had a gull-friend before.

I know you're
depressed but
don't worry,
everything will
turn out OK.

The ship suddenly lurched to one side
and Derek lost his balance, spun across the
deck like a dizzy penguin, and banged his
helmet.

(*Thor - A Viking god)

The seagull gave a squawk. "Hold on tight, Derek. Imagine you're holding on to the Princess Anka. This storm won't last much longer - out here they don't come any stronger."

"A seagull who speaks in verse!" shouted Derek as rain began to fall.

"A puffin would be worse," replied the seagull. "My name is Frank, by the way. And it's my job to keep an eye on you."

And with that he flew off, first hugging the side of the boat where the winds were lighter, then climbing into the stormy purple skies.

He called out one last time, "Look inside the lunch bag your mum packed... There could be something to help you!"

Derek opened the goatskin bag containing his lunch and in it he found two seaweed sandwiches, some salted sheep's eyeballs (tasty!), and a note!

An old Viking recipe taken from Old Ernestina's Cook Book (She was the Keith Floyd of her day)

EYEBALL DELIGHT

1. Take two sheeps' eyeballs.

2. Add Salt.

3. Eat.

(serves one).

Chapter Three: Mast of the Day - in which Frank's plan hits the deck.

By dawn the storm was over and the Viking ships made good progress across the North Sea. In a few days the shoreline of Northumbria would come into view and the attack could begin.

Chief Harald was strolling about the ship, speaking to each of his men in turn, sharing a leg of moose, slapping them on the back, and telling old Viking jokes...

The chief came and stood next to Derek.

"So, my boy, looking forward to the battle ahead?"

"Er...I wanted to talk to you about that, Chief."

And before he could change his mind, Derek thrust a piece of parchment into Chief Harald's hand. It was the note he'd found the night before.

Harald Hafnomörssy unfurled the parchment with his huge, hairy, battle-scarred hands and began to read.

As he read, his eyebrows began to quiver like two over-excited caterpillars, and eventually they met, just above the chief's nose, making an extremely annoyed expression indeed.

Harald Hafnomörssy wasn't too good at reading, but he scanned the runes* slowly, and spoke out loud as he read…

Dear Mr. Hafnomörssy,

In the name of the God Thor, I greet you. I'm very sorry, but please could you excuse Derek from the raid as he has a bit of a temperature and a sore throat.
May your sword smite its way to Valhalla.
   Yours sincerely,
   Ernestina Drodnodrott
               (Derek's Mum)

(*Runes = Viking writing. There was a saying - "Runes help you read more easily.")

The chief looked Derek in the eye.

"So... Poor Derek isn't feeling too well?"

"Not at my best, Chief. I have this ticklish cough..."

"Well, if you don't want to fight, that's all right by me."

"Well, in that case, you tin-clad tower of trauma, I suggest you get ready for the battle ahead. And you can start by shinning up that mast and keeping a look out for...for whatever look-outs look out for..."

this mast goes up quite abit further!
By the underpants of Odin! I don't fancy going up there!!!

Derek's knees turned to jelly. (Well no, they didn't really, but you know what I mean.) The mast was like the neck of an over-heated giraffe: tall, slippery, and waving around a lot.

Olaf Dednafffellur laughed like a couple of hyenas at a comedy show.

"He can't swim and he can't climb. What can he do?"

Derek gripped the mast with both arms and began to clamber up as best he could.

He didn't look down and he didn't look up until he finally reached the top.

There were jeers from the Vikings below.

I told you he watched 'Mast of the Day,' and 'Mast-ermind'... HA·HA·HA!

Fortunately Derek wasn't quite alone. Frank the seagull had joined him on top of the mast and muttered some words of encouragement.

"You've turned a strange hue,
  But look at the view..."

And there before them lay the coast of Britain, shimmering in the early morning sea-haze.

How would the raiders fare? Would Derek's nerve hold? What prices did the Britons charge for a soft drink and a sandwich??!!

Chapter Four: Battle! - in which Derek gets wet feet.

The target in this particular raid was the monastery at Holy Island (see map). There they hoped to find treasure, valuable herbs and medicines, and a blind date for the chief's brother, Leif*.

NORTHUMBRIA

WET

SCOUSE

NORTH

FEET

The island

the hole from which it gets its name

A MAP OF HOLY ISLAND AT THE TIME OF THE VIKING ATTACK (QUARTER TO NINE)

(*Leif the bald. Became chief in 943 AD, only to die after a passing bear mistook his new wig for a piece of moss.)

The monasteries were usually poorly defended because the monks didn't have swords or axes, just one or two catapults and some heavy books. Even so, there was always the chance of encountering an army of Britons, gathered to protect their shore, or even worse, a rival group of Vikings.

The boats hit the shore and with a great blood-curdling cry, the battle began. Derek began wading ashore, sword safely tucked out of the way, wondering why the water was so cold even though it was autumn.

This rubber ring looks ridiculous but these waves are dangerous!

He waved his broadsword in the air, since that was what everybody else seemed to be doing. Overhead, Frank the seagull was shouting words of encouragement. The Viking raiders quickly found a sign directing them to the monastery.

"Ignore the bit about Vikings!" shouted Chief Harald to his men. "Follow me and we'll fill our boats with high quality treasure!"

Derek found his nostrils reacting to the smell of a particularly sweaty armpit. It belonged to Olaf Dednafffellur.

You'd better bring back some valuable loot, Derek, or I'll tell the Princess what a coward you are. Hee·Hee!

Feeling even more depressed than usual, Derek watched Olaf run off in to battle, and then realised that he was the last one left on the beach. Not counting Frank the seagull.

"It's no use, Frank, my heart isn't in this battle. But then if I don't bring back a hoard of stuff I'm in big trouble."

The seagull thought for a moment.

"If you've no wish to fight and parry, then buy your loot at a cash and carry."

Derek slapped his helmet with excitement. "Of course! I've got a couple of coins in my tunic. All I have to do is find a market where I can buy some bits and pieces, then I can claim to have won them in battle. Frank, you're a genius!"

It was hard work walking up the sand-dunes in chain-mail and wearing a heavy helmet, but eventually Derek made it. After another ten minute walk he found himself by a small thatched hut, outside of which a sign read:

Derek knocked on the door of the hut and entered. A small bell rang. Two nervous monks stood against the wall in the furthest corner of the hut.

"Don't draw your sword," they called out.

How could I draw my sword? I don't have any crayons.

ETHELRED ↗

ATHELSTANE (the one ↗ with the long hair)

Ethelred and Athelstane laughed nervously.

"Don't kill us, please. You can have half price off anything in the shop."

"Twenty per cent, Ethelred."

"Sorry, twenty per cent. And free wrapping paper."

Derek smiled and took out his coins. "That's very kind, but no wrapping."

The monks breathed a sigh of relief.

"Ethelred, why don't you get the gentleman a cup of something while I show him round?"

Half an hour later, Derek emerged carrying a brooch, two necklaces, a sketch of the harbour, some pots of home-made jam, and a venerable Bede tea-towel. It had been an expensive trip, but worth every coin, or so Derek felt. Frank wasn't so sure.

"That was daylight robbery," he shrieked. "And you were the one being robbed."

"Well at least I've got something to take home. I wonder how the others are getting on?"

Some brief highlights of the battle:

Chapter Five: Hero we Go, Hero we Go - in which Derek takes the credit but feels guilty.

Amid the smoke and confusion, Derek was able to arrive back at the beach undetected. One or two Viking warriors were already beginning to appear, bloodstained, carrying stolen treasure, grinning from ear to ear.

Derek stood around a while before asking a burly beserker:

Excuse me, but can you tell me the time of the next boat back to Upper Elkshead?

It was Sven Forkbeard, one of the toughest warriors from *Serpent's Breath*.

We're leaving now, Derek, follow us. An army of Britons has arrived, the air will soon be dark with their spears.

Derek didn't fancy that.

Sven looked down at Derek's 'loot' with an admiring gaze.

"You must have fought well, Depressed Derek, to have won such finery and tasty jams. The chief will be pleased you proved yourself in battle at last."

Derek rubbed his beard, shyly. He didn't like telling tall tales. Especially not to tall Vikings. Sven Forkbeard was a giant of a man, even taller than Derek, and his sword had inflicted more cuts than a packet of *Bic* razors.

A few metres from the boat, a warning cry rang out from Chief Harald's mobile horn. The Britons' army had arrived and was running towards the beach. A spear landed uncomfortably close to Derek's foot. He was glad he'd cut his toe-nails the night before.

"Shouldn't we turn and fight?" cried out Olaf Dednafffellur.

This was the worst suggestion Derek had ever heard in his life and he hoped the chief would think so too.

A spear thumped into Derek's shield with a loud thud.

Chief Harald thought for a moment, then sounded the retreat. "Time to head for home, my boys! Head for home!"

Serpent's Breath drew quickly away from the beach, leaving the frustrated Briton warriors far behind.

Chapter Six: Soup of the Day is Elk - in which Derek finally gets home again.

For four days and four nights *Serpent's Breath* sailed back across the North Sea. The winds were kind and the stars were bright. On the fifth day, Chief Harald's warriors arrived home to find that the women and children of the village had prepared a magnificent feast for them.

← the chief always got to eat first

There was elk pie, roast elk, elk pancakes, elk soup, and Derek's favourite, elk-flavoured ice-cream.

Everyone, it seemed, had heard about Derek's achievements in battle (cough, cough) and wanted to congratulate him. His mum had told all the neighbours. Haakon the harpist had composed a special song in his honour, and worst of all, the chief himself seemed most impressed.

Princess Anka was standing next to Derek.

Can I get you a glass of beer, Derek the Daring?

"No th-th-thanks," replied Derek, with a stammer. "After a sail I usually stay off the ale."

The Princess had eyes as blue as the ice in the Fjords of Fjordhaven. Her hair was as blonde as polar bear fur.

Derek's heart began to beat faster.

"There were many who thought you would be afraid in battle, Derek Drodnodrott, but not I."

Derek blushed a little beneath his beard. He reached into his pocket and gave her the brooch he'd bought at the antique shop.

(Actual size)

At first Anka was delighted. She smiled.

"It's the most beautiful brooch I've ever seen." But then, as she examined it further, Derek suddenly realised he'd forgotten to remove the price label. Anka had seen it too.

ETHELRED
&
ATHELSTANE
ANTIQUE SHOP
8, HOLY ISLAND

Derek, you didn't win this in battle, you bought it.

Derek felt so depressed he didn't even try to think up any excuses.

"I'm sorry. I wanted to win you something in battle, but I just couldn't face it. In the end I bought the brooch and all the other stuff from two monks on the island."

Anka couldn't help but smile at Derek's hang-dog look.

"Don't worry, I won't tell anyone. Besides, it's the thought that counts. I just hope you haven't left the price on your other trophies of war. Someone might notice. Keep them talking while I go and check."

Chapter Seven: Promotion - in which Derek goes up in the world but ends up feeling down.

Chief Harald drew out his mobile horn and gave it a blow. Derek trembled at the sound.

"New dawn raiders," the chief began, "raise your cups to Derek the Daring... He who will command his own boat when next we sail."

Derek fell in to a slump. He couldn't think of anything worse than commanding his own boat. That would mean a battle at least once a week, sometimes more, especially on holiday weekends.

Olaf Dednafffellur, the chief's bodyguard, swayed to his feet and angrily crashed his axe against the table.

"No!! The next boat should have been mine! I claim the right to challenge Derek Drodnodrott in battle. Let the winner keep the boat whilst the loser loses his life. Ha-ha-ha!" (Hysterical Viking laughter.)

Almost everyone seemed to like the idea of a duel to the death between Olaf the Mad and Derek the Daring, but Derek himself felt distinctly depressed. He approached the chief on bended, wobbly knees (like Cliff Richard in concert).

"I appreciate your offer, oh great Chief Harald. But I am not worthy of such a ship. I am no great warrior, as you know. And also I have little sense of direction. I'm sure Olaf Dednafffellur would be a much better choice...I really don't mind standing down."

Uh-oh...

46

Chief Harald fingered his moustache (it contained quite a few crumbs from the elk pie), before looking down at Derek with red cheeks and an expression full of thunder.

Olaf fastened on his helmet. The one with the evil-looking eye slits and posh nose-piece.

Derek hardly had time to make a few unconvincing flourishes with his own cheap sword before his opponent let out a loud bellow and sprang towards him.

"BOING!"

One of the horns on Derek's helmet twisted and then fell off. Frank the seagull was watching from the roof of the hut, but there seemed nothing he could do. Princess Anka, too, hid her eyes.

And so the battle raged...

Until the sun set...

And the moon rose...

Derek fights back with one last great effort...

Until...

Laughing, Olaf raised his sword
in triumph...

57

Olaf had fallen into a fast-flowing river, and in his heavy armour couldn't make it back to the bank. The strong currents carried him quickly out of sight, heading for the open sea.

It was about as likely as two reindeer doing the Highland Fling, but Derek had won! Chief Harald sprang to his feet as though he was on some sort of primitive Nordic pogo stick.

"Derek has won! The boat is his!"

Princess Anka handed Derek the horn which had snapped off his helmet.

"You can't go into battle with only one horn. I've got some glue in my hut. Follow me and I'll fix it for you."

For a moment Derek smiled and felt as happy as an elk with a new set of antlers. It had been a long day, but he had survived in battle against Olaf, and the Princess seemed to like him. Maybe life wasn't so depressing after all!

And then the chief spoke once more:

"By the next moon we will sail again...To find new treasures...To slay new foes...To burn down their houses and stamp on their toes..."

Derek, you will lead the longboats. And the short ones too.

Derek smiled unenthusiastically.

Who'd be a Viking?

Frank the seagull settled on his shoulder.

the
END